The Fish On My Ear

And Other Stories

To Nicn —
I have the feeling
you might smile
at one or two of
these stories —
I hope so.

Michael J. Fleming

My best wishes
Mike
X

The Fish On My Ear And Other Stories
Michael J. Fleming

Published in Great Britain 2012 by AMMBA Publishing.

www.michaeljfleming.co.uk

Set in Garamond 11 pt.
Cover and book design by Matt Fleming.

Printed in Great Britain by Witley Press Ltd., Hunstanton, Norfolk.

ISBN 978-0-9574610-0-0

Acknowledgements

My undying gratitude goes to Beverley and the rest of Team Fleming, from the oldest (who accompanied me to my first short story award ceremony) to the youngest (who suggested the title for this collection) and all those in between who helped and encouraged me, throughout the development of this book.

Foreword

Death, whether it be sought, or sidles up unbidden, whether it be successful at first strike or fail temporarily, will of course, never be denied. For Death is the ultimate stalker, with the outcome ever certain.

Contents

Window Gazing

I could not have guessed, that so soon after slipping out of my apartment on that bright Autumn day, I would become something of a celebrity. Indeed, my first feeling was one of irresponsibility as I passed the Holt apartment, knowing at that moment the family would be sitting down to a healthy avocado salad. The Holt Saturday lunch was a confection that Grechen recommended every time she saw me creeping out to the pub. Of the four of them, Bob, Grechen and the two kids, it was only the eight year old boy who looked my way as I passed. I locked eyes with Kyle for a moment, as he was about to take a bite from his celery stick. He held it there in front of his open mouth, like a microphone. Strangely enough, years later I went to see Kyle in concert, in Brighton. By that time, Bob and Gretchen had come to terms with his career and life-style choices. It helped that Emma had qualified as a doctor and produced their two grandchildren. But it would be Kyle who cared for his parents in their declining years.

I moved on from the Holt's place and passed the apartment where old Brendan Ladd lived. Although we were long-term neighbours, I had never actually been in Brendan's home. Initially, I was surprised to see that my reclusive acquaintance had guests. But as I took in the scene, I realised that Brendan, who sat facing the window, had placed four mannequins around him. The two male mannequins were dressed in open neck shirts and jeans whilst the two females had each been adorned with dresses and wigs, one blonde, the other brunette. The party-goers appeared to be chatting with each other, giving the impression of a lively reception. Throughout the gaiety, Brendan slept peacefully, missing all the fun.

I looked up to see a lazy plane passing overhead, like a tiny brooch on a faded blue shawl. I took in the smell of coffee and warm bread from where I was heading, Mr Pannelli's delicatessen. I liked Pannelli. He was a family man and he worked hard at holding on to his regulars.

I heard a woman scream and a car screech to a halt. I wanted to turn and look in their direction but found myself unable to warrant the effort. I kept moving.

As I passed Rhea's apartment I thought, Rhea my dear, why won't you give me a chance? Why do you see other men when it is me that should be sharing that glass of wine? These thoughts were passing through my head as Rhea lifted hers. She caught my eye like a paparazzo catches his subject – unprepared and wanting.

And then I was away and approaching the Milton place, the blinds on the beautiful living room raised, permitting those passing to see the carefully chosen furniture and the tasteful decorations. I saw the Hockney and the elegant display cabinet with the pewter figurines that Maggie Milton lived only to dust. And the baby grand piano that Freddy used to play with such sensitivity. On the far wall, I saw the huge mirror. And there was me looking back at myself, eyes widened, hair streaming.

I thought how strange it was that my own face should be the final one that I would ever see.

But I had forgotten that, on the front of his delicatessen, Mr Pannelli had an awning which he openend on very sunny autumn days such as this. It was into that beautiful blue and white striped cradle that I fell, the chamois leather flying from my hand and landing with a splat at the feet of the screaming woman.

Benchmarks

Barclay

When he could no longer afford to keep the bookshop, Barclay Minnis paid off the lease. He gave Sammy, his young Saturday help, £50 as a thank-you and told him to keep in touch. He returned what stock he could and the rest he distributed amongst the charity shops in the High Street. Then he was free. At the age of fifty four, with a small pension and his own house, the world, if not his oyster that might feed him and gift him a pearl, was at least his mussel that might be gritty and give him the runs. As it turned out, it was somewhere between the two.

Barclay wanted to keep himself busy. He had always been good with his hands and decided to take a course in sign-writing. This too came easily to him and he was soon helping other students with their assignments. And one Sunday afternoon in November, Sammy knocked on the door of Barclay's small terraced house. After tea had been brewed and pleasantries exchanged, the young man came to the point.

Sammy's grandfather had passed away two months before and his mother had contracted with the Council, to provide a commemorative bench on Eastbourne's long and sweeping promenade. Now she needed an inscription etched onto the bench and could Barclay help? Barclay could, but felt he needed to know more about the deceased. And so it was arranged that Barclay would call in to see Sammy's mother Liselle, to learn a little more about her late father.

The three of them sat in Liselle's kitchen-diner and talked about old Stanley. Barclay learned that he had spent his working life, building and tuning organs. Organs in churches, chapels and theatres. Liselle had told Barclay she wanted etched onto the newly-acquired bench the words, *"Stanley Duggan, 1930-2011, who loved Eastbourne and its churches."* Barclay, whilst looking both supportive and sympathetic, had somehow conveyed a sense of unease.

'I wonder Mrs Bishop, if something like *"Stanley Duggan, 1930-2011, in tune with Eastbourne for 80 years"*, might be more in keeping?' His eyebrow stayed raised until she replied.

'Oh, that's much better. And call me Liselle, please.' Thereafter, he did. They talked about fonts and staining and the matter was settled. Sammy would help with moving the bench to Barclay's cluttered shed. A fee of £30 was agreed for Barclay's work but when the time came, he would not hear of accepting the money. A dinner invitation was the compromise.

Over the coming months, word spread of Barclay's skill. Liselle had a work-friend who also wanted a commemorative bench on the seafront. George's wife had died suddenly at home at the age of forty two. George had a friend who worked in the town hall and it was not long before the Council were pointing those who wanted to place a bench on the seafront, in Barclay's direction. George, Garth from Birmingham and Muriel from Old Town, were just three of the grieving who were grateful for Barclay's wit and wisdom.

*

George

George had always considered himself to be the support act in his marriage. It was quite obvious to everyone that Maddy was the star. She was a looker; she was one of life's fun people. She seemed to crackle with energy and friends swarmed and swooped around her like starlings in a dusk-cluster. George was happy to hover in the wings as though he was the producer of a successful show. And now Maddy had succumbed to a genetic heart malfunction that had been lying in wait all her life. A design fault in the engine that did not show its hand until she was roaring down life's fast lane.

If Barclay had not already known that George was a solicitor, he would have guessed. Tall and too stooped for a man of forty five, George was still dressed for work when Barclay called around to his house on the agreed evening. His grey suit jacket was hanging on the back of a dining chair and his black spotted tie was coiled like a tropical snake on the desert of a table.

'Thanks for coming round to discuss this Barclay,' said George from the edge of his armchair's seat. 'Thinking about this bench thing has been a big help.'

Barclay smiled and looked beyond George to the open kitchen door and the pile of unwashed dishes cluttering the work surface 'That's quite alright George. I'm so sorry for your loss but glad to help if I can. Now, have you had time to think about what you might want inscribed on the bench?'

George pulled a face as though this was the final and most difficult question in a quiz show. 'Well, I have been thinking, but I can't really come up with anything that would fit. All my ideas would take up ten benches! There is just so much to say.'

'Perhaps you might like to tell me one or two things about Maddy. I may be able to help,' said Barclay.

And so George described Maddy's work as a Personal Trainer: how she often met her clients on the seafront to put them through their programmes; how she was also a great homemaker; how it had been her decision not to have children; the way that other men ogled her and women loved her. Barclay nodded sympathetically throughout.

After a halting discussion as to the wording of the inscription, Barclay said,

'George, do you think that Madeleine might have liked *"Madeleine Jarman, 1969 - 2011. Ran To Live, Ran To Life, Ran To George"*?'

'She'd like that Barclay, she'd like that a lot,' said George. And that is what Maddy Jarman got.

*

Garth

Garth Spennymore telephoned Barclay one evening in June. He explained in his strong Birmingham accent, that he would like Barclay to buy a bench, put an inscription on it and negotiate with the Council to place it on the seafront. As if reading from a fast-food menu, he gave Barclay his late mother's details. Garth would send enough money in advance to cover the cost.

'I can do all that Mr Spennymore, but the key information is the wording of the inscription. What would sum your mother up?'

'Look mate, Mum left instructions in her will for all this. And the money. So the inscription isn't really important. So you choose. Alright?'

Barclay was thinking Garth's accent might be useful for cutting through a hardwood bench leg he was working on. 'Well, I can suggest some wording, but I need to know something about Joan; what her interests were; why she liked Eastbourne.'

A deep sigh came from the other end of the phone as though Garth had just been told that the double cheeseburger with fries was off. 'Look, all I know is that she went to Eastbourne twice a year. June and December. She absolutely loved the place. Used to go on

and on about it. She stayed at the Cavendish
Hotel. She went with the Edgbaston Seniors
Club. Now I'll stick a cheque in the post.'

'Hang on Mr Spennymore, could you tell me
about the club. What did she do there?'

'It don't really matter what she did there, it's
got bugger-all to do with the bench.' Barclay
did not reply. He let the silence build. Garth
let out another sigh. 'Okay, she was the Events
Secretary. Looked after their bridge matches,
organised their day-trips and their summer
break. Stuff like that.'

'So, she would have known the people at the
Cavendish? And the Coach company?'

After making the phone calls and dropping
in at the Cavendish, Barclay came up with his
inscription. Three weeks later, on a Sunday
morning in July, Garth Spennymore sat on the
recently-installed bench facing the sea. The
inscription visible to the passer-by read:

*"Joan Spennymore, 1933-2011, who loved
Eastbourne"*

Garth was a big man with a dark moustache and a pony tail drawn from the scrapings of what was left of his hair. At that moment, although the sea sparkled and the pebbly beach was a riot of colourful picnic encampments, Garth's mind was elsewhere. He was thinking of himself as a young boy, playing in the park in Edgbaston, running between slide and swing, waving to his Mum who sat on a bench, waving back. He did not notice the people strolling by who looked askance at this big man, with his moist eyes, smiling in solitude. When after an hour Garth rose to leave, he revealed the full inscription on the bench:

"Joan Spennymore, 1933-2011, who loved Eastbourne almost as much as she loved her own dear son."

*

Muriel

Muriel said that her husband Roland had died in his favourite chair: the one by the big screen in the betting shop on Terminus Road. It was a punch-line Barclay knew she must have used before, because she leaned forward in her armchair and, with obvious expectation, awaited the look of embarrassed shock on Barclay's face. As soon as he obliged, she threw her head back and laughed.

'He was a case my Roly,' she said with undisguised affection. 'He always got out from under my feet while I pottered with the housework. He was in that betting shop every day of the week, bless him. Only ever took £10 with him usually, but of course, it was Grand National day…' Her voice trailed off.

Roland had put £20 on the favourite in the Grand National. His horse had gone on to win, but Roland never knew that. He had keeled over when his horse was two fences from home with a two furlong lead. Apparently the staff and customers had fallen silent when Roland had hit the floor, and someone claiming to know CPR had gone to work on Roland's chest to the wild commentary from the loudspeakers. When the medics arrived they knew Roland would never be picking up his winnings. Not in person. The betting shop manager delivered them to Muriel, together with the product of a whip-round from the other regulars. Muriel had decided to spend the money on a seafront bench. For the first ten years or so of their married lives, it was where she and Roland used to stroll on Saturday afternoons, before the betting shop stole him away.

'Can you think of something witty Mr Minnis? Roly was the life and soul of that betting shop. He was a hoot. Go on, surprise me!'

Barclay and Sammy were installing Roland's bench early one Thursday morning. Something witty Muriel had said. Now Barclay stood back to examine the inscription:

"Roland Knowle 1949-2011, Always a Stable Influence."

If the breeze had been blowing southerly instead of westerly; if Barclay had not stepped back at that precise moment from the bench; if the guy on the bike had had the foresight to call-out, things would have been different. But none of those circumstances arose. Instead, the cyclist hit Barclay blind, sending him sideways like a giant sandbag falling off a tailgate.

Whilst the cyclist was still airborne, he heard the crack that he discovered later, was the sound of Barclay's head hitting the arm of the bench. Barclay died in Eastbourne hospital the following day. Liselle and Sammy were at his bedside.

*

Liselle and Sammy

That evening, Liselle was inconsolable. She had not known Barclay for many months, but she had recognised him as a man she would soon love deeply. They had enjoyed many evenings together, sometimes with Sammy over a lazy family-style dinner at Liselle's house; sometimes as a couple at Barclay's. On their fourth evening at Barclay's house, they had become intimate. For each of them, it was their first relationship since their respective divorces. They had not needed to spell anything out for Sammy. He knew their arrangement and the three of them had been developing their positions; mother, son and new-man-on-scene; marking their ground and happy to redefine boundaries as little pressures emerged or eased.

Barclay's funeral was delayed by the inquest, but Sammy knew straight away what he needed to be working on. As soon as he told his mother, she was uplifted. It wasn't a big thing in itself, but it was so right, so apposite, that she threw herself into the project. She spoke to George, Sammy contacted Muriel and Garth. They split another six between them. Everyone was delighted to contribute to a commemorative bench for Barclay.

Sammy looked down at the low cliffs that tumbled to Holywell beach and the sea. His gaze turned slowly eastwards taking in, beyond the thin line of conifers, the expanse of English Channel, today sparkling under a bright sky. His eye followed the horizon through to the distant cliffs of Hastings and then dropped down to the pier in the mid-distance, protruding like an arm into the sea, as though Eastbourne was indicating it wanted to turn right. The smile that had appeared on his face, widened into a grin and he began shaking his head as if disabusing a friend of their understandable, but sadly incorrect, proposition. 'Barclay,' he said aloud to himself 'this is the spot for you my friend. We both know you'll just love it.'

With his arm outstretched along its backrest, he gently patted the finely rounded top of Barclay's Bench. He shifted around to look again at the inscription that he had proposed and the others had cheered:

"Barclay Minnis 1956-2012. Provided A Benchmark For So Many Lives."

The Fish On My Ear

Scruffy Murphys sits back from the beach and the cycle path in the East Coast Park. From its rickety deck you can sit with a cold beer and watch the world go by. About the best time to do this is any afternoon in February. Which is why I am here. At this time, the temperature in Singapore is not so hot as to deter the cyclists and joggers; the skateboarders and the walkers; the mums on their bikes towing, with long twisted beach towels, kids on scooters. Beyond the cycle path and the beach, a multitude of boats idle on the sea. Perhaps waiting for a cargo to be loaded or unloaded. Or for a legal wrangle to be resolved and free them to get back to shifting goods around the oceans.

I have with me my battered copy of *Les Liaisons dangereuses* and am about to start Letter 163, when the man standing at the smoking area, turns to face me. He stubs out his cigarette in the large ash-can and smiles. He is tall enough to carry his rounded belly with some elegance and has a bald head which, I'm somehow sure, would sport an afro hair style if nature allowed. Now he walks to my table.

'Good day sir. I hope I am not disturbing you but wondered if I might introduce myself. I am Harry.' He extends a large, strong hand which I accept whilst attempting to identify his accent. Central American? Caribbean?

'I would like to inquire about the fish on your ear?'

'Excuse me?'

'The fish on your ear. I wonder if we may discuss its… origin?'

'Well, where do people normally acquire tatts but in a tattoo parlour?' I know as soon as I speak, that my tone is unreasonably sharp.

His face takes on a slightly pained expression as though he has swallowed back down something eaten earlier. 'If it is indeed a tattoo, I fear I may be addressing the wrong person. But my friend,' he lowers his voice and leans towards me, 'I am hoping you will confide in me and confirm that the fish is not a tattoo.'

It is true that the fish on my ear is a birth-mark. Until this moment, I had been certain that only my parents, my sister and I had known of this. It had been a smudge at birth that within weeks had formed into a perfect fish-shape of the type that might be seen in any children's colouring book. My parents had claimed to have had my infant earlobe tattooed on a family trip to the Irish Republic, in a village the name of which they could not recall. As a boy it had attracted much attention with the teasing easily outweighed by the admiration and envy of my peers. I will need to talk to my sister tonight.

'Harry, I'm sitting having a quiet read and a cold beer. Really, I'd just like some space please. If you don't mind?'

Harry slowly unbuttons the sleeve of his blue floral shirt and pushes it back to reveal on his right forearm the perfect depiction of a scorpion. 'This is not a tattoo either. Like yours, it is a birth-mark.'

I study his arm. 'Ridiculous. That has to be a tattoo. Now come on Harry, leave me alone, there's a good chap.'

'It is as much a birth-mark as yours my friend. We are two of twelve so blessed.'

'What are you saying?'

'I am saying that, as well as you and I, there are ten other people with zodiac sign birth-marks. We twelve are spread throughout the world.'

'Harry, do I look like a fool? Please…'

Harry stops me by placing his forefinger on his lips. 'Let me explain.' And he proceeds to tell his story.

Before meeting me, he had already met three of the others: a young Iraqi man with the Gemini twins birthmark on his right calf; a middle-aged Japanese lady with the crab of Cancer on her neck and Carlos, an elderly Uruguayan man whose lower back sported a perfect lion birth-mark. The last of these had in his time, also met four others of what he called the zodians. The old man had believed four was a record. The location of each of his four zodians had been revealed to him in dreams. Harry confirmed that he too had had a dream for each of those he had visited.

'So Harry, you had a dream about me? And you're telling me that somewhere else on this earth there's someone with… a set of scales as a birth-mark?' I chuckle at the image, but Harry is unmoved and holds up a hand to signify he is about to carry on with his story. At that moment the waitress swings by and, without consulting me, Harry orders two beers. He continues.

'The thing you need to understand is that there can only be twelve of us.'

I look Harry up and down. His floral shirt is complemented by khaki shorts to the knee and rope sandals. He fits right in. 'Where are you from Harry?' I ask.

'I am from an island called Eleuthera, in the

Bahamas. It is a little like Singapore must have been many years ago. But at home we do not have the... distractions you enjoy here.' He turns away from me and stares out at the iron-flat sea and the array of boats at anchor, whose only common purpose appears to be to maintain their state of inactivity.

'What kind of distractions?'

'My country is poor compared to Singapore. In Eleuthera, our roads and harbours are designed to meet the needs of the islanders. Peace is easy to come by. Here life is one of aeroplanes swooping and taxis roaring and people hurrying to important meetings. And ships that arrive but do not seem to leave.'

'So what occupies you in Eleuthera, Harry?'

'Life is simple. I am a fisherman. It is true that I also own a hotel, but in my heart I am a fisherman first. I have a small boat and with my brothers I fish for grouper, snapper, parrotfish. We gather conch for chowders and salads. When we fish, we rely only on celestial navigation which we learned from our father, as he had learned from his.' He now turns his gaze back to me.

'We believe that the stars shine to guide us, rather than to cast a light on our indiscretions. You should try it my friend.'

I am about to challenge the aspersion, if indeed that is what it is, when in her white top and black trousers, the waitress returns with our beers. Harry slaps a fifty on the tray and waves her away. She is clearly thrilled and the wooden deck that had rumbled under the weight of her arrival, is untroubled as she floats back to the bar. Harry seems not to notice the effect of his largess.

'But hang on a moment Harry, there must be a mistake. I don't even live in Singapore. I am visiting my sister. She has worked here for years, but I come from England where right now it's freezing cold, wet, windy... horrible. So I don't see how you could have had a dream about me being here.'

I am thinking I really must talk to Lauren when she returns from work, whatever hour that might be. Some nights over this past two weeks, she has not returned from the bank until midnight. She certainly earns that fat salary. Could she have talked to someone at work about me? We went out for drinks with a few of them last Friday night. But no one struck me as odd.

'But Harry, assuming that you are right about this birth-mark business, why do we have them? Are we supposed to be some sort of club? What is the point?'

'We do not know the answer to those questions. I spent some time discussing these matters with Carlos when I met him in Montevideo. It is possible that twelve zodians have played a role since the dawn of Hellenistic astronomy. Maybe even back to Babylonian astronomy. Our best guess is that we are the unwitting guardians of our Zodiac signs.'

This puzzles me. I have no connections with fishing or conservation nor of marine biology. Now it is Harry's turn to chuckle. 'You are thinking you are not an ichthyologist, so in what way might you be a guardian? We simply do not know my friend.' He sees my look of puzzlement shift to one of inquiry.

'Ichthyology my friend. The study of fish,' he explains as though to a child. I understand.

'So, why not get those of us together who you know of? We could have a little conference - assuming we could communicate. There must be, what, eight you could contact. Then we could share stories. See if there is a common thread to help understand what this is all about.' Harry grows serious. He slides my beer towards me and holds his glass up as in a toast. I realise that my throat is parched. We clink glasses and drink. Mine disappears almost in one long draught.

'Language has never been a barrier in my experience,' said Harry. 'However, we cannot meet because I am afraid all the people that Carlos had met have passed away. As have those that I have met, including Carlos. They have been replaced by others. One day, one of them will have a dream about me and come calling.'

'Perhaps that will be me Harry, a trip to Eleuthera sounds fun.' I am picturing myself on a deserted beach, shoeless in the hot sand, a conch shell in one hand, a miraculously cold beer in the other.

Harry is shaking his head. 'It will not be you my friend.'

'How could you know that, Harry?'

'Because at 2.45pm local time today, a baby girl will be born in the Ukraine. She will have a birth-mark in the shape of a fish on her right earlobe. And there can only be twelve of us.'

I look at my watch. It is 2.44pm. I hear a soft thud as my book hits the wooden deck. The calling of the children on their bikes and skateboards fades. The boats moored in the middle distance become black smudges on a dark blue flag. The vague outline of Harry rises from the chair and walks away. I close my eyes.

Peace.

A Civil Affair

Guilt is corrosive. Like acid, it eats by layers and in so doing, reduces and wracks its host. So it was with Lemmy's son-in-law, Maxwell Jones. In the matter of the accident, he had been blameless. There were no charges and the press had conferred upon him the anonymity of 'The 35 year-old man driving the silver Saab.' Maxwell and Gail had wanted to attend the funeral, to offer deep condolences, to show their grief, to allow Maxwell to explain, but the little girl's family had denied them. They had insisted that there be no contact. No phone call, no letter. By the time of the inquest, Maxwell's guilt had overpowered him and the Police supported his request not to appear in person. So another chance to bow his head in sorrow in front of the girl's parents, had slipped by like a leaf in the wind. And Lemmy came to realise that Maxwell had freedom without forgiveness; innocence without absolution.

For Lemmy kept a watchful eye on his son-in-law, always aware that the well-being of his daughter and grandson was tied into Maxwell's future. Or should be. It was the main reason he had brought forward his retirement date. Now, two years after the accident, Maxwell and Gail were the senior partners in The L. E. Morton Engineering Consultancy, their elevation from Heads of Department, a parting gift to his only daughter and her husband from Lemmy. Leo Edward Morton, Lemmy to all who knew him. Founder of the company and legend to all who worked there. Lemmy, the mixer and fixer; the boss on whose beaming face no employee had wanted to place a look of disappointment; the jazz-playing crooner who lit up the works party; the man everybody other than Maxwell, hoped would walk through the door and say that his retirement announcement last year, had been a practical joke; the person who had retained the company's assets in his own name.

For as well as his charm, Lemmy had a nose for business that was sharper than any of his £1,000 suits. He had been both strategist and day-to-day problem-solver; a creator and a shirt-sleeved doer. He would have been the complete all-rounder had the compulsion to apply his magnificent powers of persuasion and diplomacy, on occasion, not outweighed his judgment. For it was his suggestion that Gail should work from home. He had feared that when he retired, the little office squabbles between his daughter and her husband, would likely grow, to no one's advantage. But he hadn't bargained for the marginalising effect being away from the office would have on her. How, despite his black moods, it was to Maxwell rather than Gail, that staff would inevitably refer, no matter the reporting line, the power of the email or the efficacy of the video-conference.

And Lemmy knew that the problems in their marital landscape were not caused solely by the road accident. Indeed not. Although that terrible occurrence was clearly the biggest mountain, Lemmy knew it was part of a range. No one either mentioned or had forgotten Maxwell's self-confessed one-nighter at the Birmingham Civil Engineer's conference when Gail was eight month's pregnant with Mo. Maxwell, with his brilliance, who could keep the firm in work, but couldn't keep his mouth shut. Maxwell who carried his guilt like a tour-guide carries aloft a pennant on a cane. Maxwell the martyr, guilty until proven innervated thought Lemmy, as he took Gail's mid-afternoon tea into her study. 'Tea as ordered, with milk, stirred anti-clockwise by a left-handed Lancashire lad,' said Lemmy through a newly-planted, beaming smile.

'Thanks Dad, where's Morton?'

'The blonde bomber has bombed upstairs to get changed. School-bag and blazer hurled onto the floor with enviable gusto, as per usual.'

'Can you stay for a few minutes Dad? I want to have a quick word about Maxwell. He's in such a bad place right now what with the anniversary of the accident looming.' Lemmy nodded. 'He's worse than ever. It kills him that he has never been allowed to contact that poor girl's parents to offer his condolences.' Gail said this without irony or malice. Lemmy put his arm around her slender shoulders.

'Don't you worry love. We'll think of something to bring him round,' he said softly and with a

show of confidence that did not gain a grain of
substance until he was driving home.

*

Lemmy asked Maxwell and Gail to make sure
they had enough time for coffee and biscuits
when they came to pick up young Morton on
Saturday after his piano lesson. Eleven year old
Morton, Mo to Maxwell, though never to Gail,
was showing quite a bit of promise. Lemmy
would email him each Friday and tell him what
biscuits he had bought for the following day, as
a reward for completing his homework. That
Friday evening the email had read "Leo Edward
Morton is pleased to announce that, following
Beethoven's Minuet in G played by Master
Morton Jones, on Saturday 14th May 2011,
Jammy Dodgers will be served." Mo knew that
Jammy Dodgers was code for Jerry Lee Lewis
and that his granddad would show him the left
hand bass line he so wanted to learn. Last week
it had been Bourbons and Billy Joel. The week
before, Lemon Wafers and Leon Russell.

The lesson had gone well, for Mo had indeed
worked hard on Beethoven and Lemmy was

a fine tutor. To Lemmy it had always seemed to be a case of understanding the architecture of music. Now he cherished the time that retirement had given him to sit and play alone most afternoons for an hour or so. Debussy, he loved Debussy. But he missed those odd occasions at the firm when he was expected to play at any celebration that took place down at the King's Head. For Bill Cumming's leaving do in 2009 when Bill actually stood on the piano to sing "Delilah"; and a year earlier at Joan's leaving party, before she went off to marry that chap from Jersey, when Lemmy actually crooned his way through a Billy Joel ballad, changing the lyric to "Always a P.A to Me."

This Saturday afternoon in May was warm, with a sky uncluttered by cloud. The smell of roses and sweet-peas wafted across the patio and the white linen curtain on the french window fluttered like a flag. The sound of Mo working his way through an extra half hour of Beethoven in the music room, could not detract from the beauty of the setting.

'I love this garden Dad,' said Gail. 'I wish Mum was still here to enjoy it with us.'

'We all do dear. On days like this I often fancy I hear her humming Bizet as she dead-heads the roses.' Lemmy paused and allowed his gaze to wander across the flower beds. Then as though he had just remembered an urgent appointment, he slapped his thighs and turned to Maxwell. 'Happy, happy days. But look, I have an idea I want to put to you. I think it would be helpful if I visited Mr and Mrs Day and told them how, for the last two years, you have been respecting their wishes not to make contact. But they need to know that you're dreadfully sorry. They must realise Maxwell, that the little girl's death has been weighing on your mind the whole time. That you want their forgiveness. That you would like to visit them in person.' Lemmy sat back and bestowed a benefactor's smile. 'What do you think?'

Maxwell had grown ashen. He glared at Gail but she was busy assessing the strength of her coffee. Her denim-clad legs were crossed and wrapped again at the ankle as though she were chilly on this warm, early-summer day.

'Well, I've never mentioned to you Lemmy, just how much this has been affecting me. But I guess it's hard to hide this sort of thing from the most insightful man I've ever met.' Lemmy beamed while Gail fiddled with an ear-ring. 'But to tell you the truth Lemmy, it's just not on. It's something only I can do when I'm ready. And that's not going to be anytime soon. So I don't want you going anywhere near Mr and Mrs Day. Please. I hope you understand.' Lemmy's beam had slowly transformed into a thoughtful purse, as though he had popped a small olive branch into his mouth and was not sure whether to chew it or swallow it whole. Gail was staring over Maxwell's head at the distant line of leylandii, which waved in a sudden gust, as though hailing castaways on a shore.

*

Lemmy thought that the groans of the bark and sawdust under his feet, as he picked his way up the path to the Day's house, would herald his arrival. But the place remained silent as he peered into the porch in search of a bell. For he had weighed Maxwell's wishes carefully, but decided that his plan was indeed the best one. Maxwell would soon see that his old father-in-law had got this one pitch perfect. Lemmy had chosen a mid-grey business suit and had off-set the crispness of his white shirt, with a flecked, black and grey tie. He had been to enough meetings in his time to know that what you wore was how you were. And he wanted to strike just the right tone: sombre, smart, trustworthy.

A cobweb stretched from the corner of the porch to a sign on the window ledge which announced that "We are in the garden!" The porch floor was bedecked with withered leaves that cracked underfoot as he stepped in to knock on the door. He knocked again and then, cupping his hands around the side of his head, put his face to the dark-blue glazing panel. He heard footsteps on the staircase. Lemmy stood back and straightened up, composing his face into an expression conveying the gravitas he felt would cover all the bases. He needed to establish his credentials, be clear in his message and be empathetic. No problem. The door opened to reveal a slightly-built woman in her late thirties, her face pretty despite the pallor of her skin. The denim dungarees and a railwayman's cap completed the impression of a doll left out in the rain.

'Hello Mrs Day. You don't know me, but my name is Leo Morton, I own a Civil Engineering practice in Uckfield, but I am calling on behalf of my son-in-law, Maxwell Jones.' He opened his mouth to continue but was halted by the look on Rebecca Day's face.

'On behalf of Max?' She said with a catch in her voice. Lemmy's mouth was still forming the shape that would allow him to say, why yes indeed, when she continued. 'How did he find me? How did he find out about Emma?'

Lemmy had been in many situations where the unexpected had cropped up; meetings where an affable colleague had lost all control with no apparent cause; negotiations where the opposition had pulled a rabbit out of the hat. The old hand knew how to tread water while he searched for salvation.

'I'm sorry if this is not a good time Mrs Day, but I think…' She cut him off.

'There's never a good time Mr Morton. And if you know about Emma, you know there never will be.' As she said this, a single tear formed in the corner of her eye and sat there as though choosing which of several paths to flow down. Her lips turned downwards and then inward as though evening-out freshly applied lipstick. Lemmy half-reached for the handkerchief in the breast pocket of his jacket, but realised that he may never find such a close match to his tie again. Instead, he took from his trouser pocket, a perfectly folded linen handkerchief which in Rebecca Day's hand, seemed to acquire the quality of a restorative. For no sooner had she wiped her face and nose than she regained her composure and spoke to Lemmy in an altogether sterner tone.

'What exactly does Max want Mr Morton?'

An exponent of mime by experience, Lemmy Morton raised his eyebrows and cocked his grey-haired head to one side, 'Might it be easier if I came inside Mrs Day?'

She held his gaze for what seemed to Lemmy, to be sufficient time to devise the basic design for a foot-bridge over the road behind him. Then Rebecca Day nodded and stood to one side as he entered the hallway.

While Rebecca made tea in the kitchen, Lemmy sat on the lounge sofa, surveying the room for little conversational toe-holds on which to build a rapport. Ornaments, paintings, photographs. When she came in with the tray, he was looking at the family photo on the dresser. The little blonde-haired girl with her blonde-haired Mum and swarthy Dad. Three Musketeers, like Gail and Maxwell and Mo.

'Tom and I got divorced a year after Emma was killed,' she said softly.

'I'm so sorry Mrs Day. I can't imagine your pain. I really did not come here to add to your distress.' He was hugely relieved that Rebecca was happy to sit in silence for a while, as they drank their tea. Eventually she spoke.

'Look, I don't know how he found me, but from the day I told him about the pregnancy, I wanted nothing to do with Max. I've had no contact with him whatsoever these last nine years and I really don't want to open up any more of the past. Tom went back to the Midlands without ever knowing he wasn't Emma's real father. He still doesn't and I want it to stay that way.' She withdrew Lemmy's handkerchief from her pocket and dabbed her nose as though her resolve required another boost from its curative properties.

Lemmy's expression was now openly betraying the struggle between empathy and confusion as Rebecca pressed on. 'I don't know how Max found out about Emma's accident, but I didn't need his sympathy when I was with Tom and I don't want it now. So please tell him that from me.'

She paused, awaiting confirmation that Lemmy would pass on this emphatic decision. But Lemmy was still computing information. Pregnancy? Nine years? He looked again at the family photograph on the dresser, studying the face of the little blonde girl. A little blond bomber. Realisation arrived like a fat and heavy stone thrown from a cliff. A dead landing. Instant traction.

*

As he trudged back down the path, Lemmy saw the mound of freshly-worked earth at the

MICHAEL J. FLEMING

front of the garden and realised that a sizeable tree must have stood there until recently. A light rain had started to fall. As he turned out of the gate, he almost lost his footing on a piece of freshly-cleaved bark, his arms for a moment flailing the air. He resisted the urge to look around to check whether Rebecca Day had witnessed his inelegant slip. Once back in the car, he sat silently, turning over in his mind what Rebecca had said. What he had seen. Beginning to plan what words he might employ for Gail and Maxwell.

The drips of rain, percolating through the tree overhead, landed on the car roof to an improvised beat. A grey pigeon fluttered down onto the bonnet of his car and stared in at him cocking his head from side to side, as though Lemmy, sitting there in his grey suit and flecked tie, might be a distant relative. A second bird followed some moments later and began to flirt unashamedly with her partner. The two of them only flapped away when he started the engine. In one sweep, the wipers cleared the rain spatterings from his windscreen and allowed him to pull away safely onto the rural road that led away from Rebecca Day's house.

He knew then that he would find no words for Gail and Maxwell. That to speak of what he knew would not be to inform, but to destroy. For there is a point, where guilt becomes terminal.

Augustus, Hadrian and Me

'How do you two boys fancy joining me on a little trip to Italy?' I said, my intercession triggering a tableau moment, with the forefinger that Uncle Adrian had been gently wagging at his brother, now hanging in the air as though he were about to fire an imaginary gun and my Dad open-mouthed, holding a napkin to his chest, as if it might stop the bullet. After a moment, Dad opened his arms in a papal pose, the napkin now a flag of peace. 'We can't take a holiday now, Laura. There's too much to do for a start. And anyway, it just wouldn't look right after all that's happened.'

What had happened was that my Nan had died two weeks before and her cremation service had taken place yesterday. It was the first time that I had ever stepped inside the crematorium chapel and I had felt immediately relieved. In the small space, the twenty or so mourners,

Nan's few relatives and near neighbours, would appear to be a good turnout.

My early role in the proceedings had been straightforward. I had ensured that everyone had an Order of Service and agreed with old neighbours I had not seen for years, that I had indeed grown. I had thanked those who said that I had my mother's fine features, my father's dark eyes and a little of my uncle's angularity. Almost all of them asked me to pass on their condolences to Dad and Uncle Adrian, seeming to overlook that I too had lost someone dear to me. Someone irreplaceable. Not for the first time, I had wished for cousins of my own age. Only Mrs Barber who lived next door to Nan, had shown me any real concern. I had met her many times when she was having lunch at Nan's and knew them to be both companion and confidante to each other. I had come to learn that the look of surprise on Mrs Barber's face was her natural countenance. That she was neither shocked nor confused when asked by Nan to pass me another slice of Battenberg.

'I haven't got over it yet dear,' she said, her hand resting on my arm and her wide and watery eyes misting up yet further. 'But she is in a good place now. She loved you to bits Laura. You know that don't you?'

'Yes I do Mrs Barber. And I thought the world of her too.' And at that moment I was back in Nan's house during my school holidays: reading aloud from a reference book to Nan whilst she loaded her home made chutney onto structurally unsound lunch crackers. I could hear Nan disagreeing with the learned author's interpretation of political life in ancient Rome. Reminding me it was my duty to go to University. And then later, Nan at my graduation sitting between Mum and Dad. Me walking across the podium to collect my degree, picking them out in the audience only because Nan's smile was like a torch in a cupboard.

Mrs Barber patted my arm and made her way down the short aisle with the other neighbours, her progress more vertical movement than forward motion, wanting to give the impression she was gaining on the other elderly mourners. It brought to mind an infirmary, where the limping and bowed each made their own search for somewhere to rest their weary frames.

Gus and Adrian, or as they were Christened, Augustus and Hadrian, carried things off with great sensitivity. Nan would have been proud too. Wiping his face and palms with a handkerchief, Dad had stepped up to deliver his eulogy. He had placed his notes on the lectern and begun by telling us how his Mum, when she had fallen pregnant, had given up a place to study Ancient History at Trinity College, Dublin. He talked of their childhood, how they used their full given names until they started school and how quickly they became aware that their names stood them apart from others. How it would take the best part of five years before they could get their mother to use the anglicised versions. I was a little distracted by Dad's left hand which, though dropped at his side, kept opening and closing, as if he were a magician showing us he was concealing nothing. He told us how as a family without a father figure, the two boys had had to take on more responsibility. How they looked after themselves while their Mum did her evening job. It was a sober point on which to hand over to his brother and the chapel remained silent as they exchanged places.

When Adrian had stepped up to the lectern,
it was obvious he was physically more
comfortable than Dad had been. He was tall
and clutched both sides of the lectern as an
evangelist might before delivering a reading on
the merits of temperance when the price of
spirits has just been slashed. But as my uncle
told us of a summer holiday the three of
them had taken to Pompeii, I could see that
his emotional comfort was nowhere near as
robust as his physical strength. It was when he
was recounting how Nan, without telling the
boys, had saved up for two years to afford the
holiday, that his voice first caught, as though
it had been snagged by a wire in the tale. He
told how she had marvelled at the sign in Latin,
urging would-be visitors to one preserved
villa to *"Beware of the Dog"* and bought one as
a souvenir. When he told us *"Cave Canem"*
was still on the gate outside her little terraced
cottage, even though she had never owned a
dog, he had to remove his glasses and wipe his
eyes with what until that point, had been a crisp
handkerchief. It was a side of my lovely uncle,
that I had always known to be there, but saw
too little of. Mrs Barber started what she hoped
would be a round of applause but nobody else

took it up and she stopped abruptly, both hands apart in mid-air as though she were winding wool. As always, she had looked surprised.

*

Dad and Adrian had chosen the hymns and I had chosen the readings. I had thought carefully about what I might say, but the two works I had chosen needed little more than the briefest introduction, saving me from displaying more emotion than Nan would have wanted.

The mourners had remained completely silent as I read the first, James Joyce's *"At That Hour"*. As I moved on to my second reading, the riffling of the two sheets of paper in my hands, seemed to fill the chapel like swords clashing.

'All of you will know that my Nan was passionate about Ancient Rome and devoted much of her time to scholarly works on the subject. So this second reading is attributed to the Roman poet Lucretius and is called *"Song for the Departed"*.'

I caught Dad and Adrian offering tight smiles of encouragement.

"And we shall sing in voices shored,
By steel and by fond reflection,
Of a comrade true and strong,
Who lent his strength,
When ours was sapped,
And gave us hope,
When ours had fled.
And we shall sing not through our tears,
But through the strength that he bequeathed."

The Humanist conducting the service had concluded with a few fine words about a woman he had never met and then we all endured the curtain and conveyor moment in our own ways. Bowed heads, silent farewells but no tears from the three of us in the front row. Just as Nan would have wanted.

*

And then yesterday afternoon back here at the hotel after the service, Augustus, Hadrian and me had played host to a handful of relatives and some of Nan's friends and neighbours. Set against the aquamarine-papered walls of the small function room, were occasional tables bearing vases of freshly-cut flowers, bowls of fruit and plates of sandwiches so thin and fine, they might have been cut by a cardsharp. We had stood in small clusters on the deep blue carpet, turning the room into a mourners' archipelago. The room was small enough to pick-up all of the conversations taking place and, whilst I spoke with two of Nan's old work colleagues, I found myself tuning in and out of all the other chatter.

Joan and Vera had worked with Nan at her final full-time job in the library. Although Nan could easily have qualified as a librarian, she was happy to be employed, like her two old friends, as an assistant.

'She didn't want the worry of ordering stock and dealing with the Council on funding and staffing. Nothing bureaucratic,' said Joan through a set of teeth that had clearly consumed some of the watercress garnish as well as a significant portion of her retirement lump-sum.

'Oh, no,' chipped in Vera. She leaned forward and lowered her voice as though entrusting me with a terrible secret. 'Your Nan loved advising people on books. She used to like to see what they were reading. Sometimes she would encourage them to move on to harder reads. But as long as people were reading and the library was busy, she was happy.' Having finished sharing her insights, Vera straightened up again. As she did so, I had feared some skeletal component was going to crack loudly and was relieved when she achieved a state of perpendicular without mishap.

Adrian was to my right, cloistered with Mrs Barber and three bust-to-bust lady dancing partners from Nan's Tuesday club. The four ladies had formed a semi-circle before my uncle as though gathered to admire a particularly fine statue.

'Yes ladies,' I heard Adrian say, 'I would encourage everyone to make a will. If any of you haven't, you should do so without delay.' Seeing by the widened eyes and slackened jaws of his audience, that his words had caused a certain amount of consternation, he went on quickly, 'Not of course, that any of you would be requiring an executor any time soon.' The collective sigh of love and relief caused Adrian to take a quarter step back.

Dad was to my left, in a knot with Mum, Auntie Audrey and Mr Jarrett, Nan's ancient and reclusive neighbour with the wayward hands. The ladies were clearly amused that Dad had thought it necessary to station himself close by in the event Mr Jarrett became too tactile. Both Mum and Auntie Audrey had said, as ex-wives, they would have felt awkward attending the service, but both agreed that the simple reception afterwards was something that their late mother-in-law would have wanted them to attend. I thought they were mistaken. Nan would have been delighted to know her two ex-daughters-in-law had supported her sons at their mother's cremation. I picked up their conversation when old Mr Jarrett was speaking.

'I knew your mother well,' he said to Gus while looking at Auntie Audrey. 'She knew her heart-rate was too high but did nothing about it. My heart-rate, by contrast, is low for my age. May I?'

He took Auntie Audrey's hand and placed it on his chest. Audrey said later she was sure that, at the moment of contact, a small dust-cloud had been released from Mr Jarrett's tweed jacket. It was when he had enquired about Audrey's heart -rate that Dad had intervened and steered Mr Jarrett away in the general direction of the cheeses.

And it had been mid-afternoon, in that calming bubble of a function room, that Mum and Auntie Audrey, had stood with their ex-husbands and me, the only off-spring. The last in line. We five had chatted more easily than any of us had dared hope. We broke into bouts of wistful laughter throughout the story of the suitcase and the bureau. Each one of us chipping in the next bit of the story as it unfolded like a cherished Persian rug. The five of us in Adrian's car on the way to the south coast, Dad beside him "navigating". Twelve year old me squashed between Mum and Auntie Audrey in the back. The three of us piled up with the bags that wouldn't fit into a boot that was already crammed with suitcases and red wine. Singing along to Elton John and Stevie Wonder. Stopping at the service area for fuel. The ladies finding the craft fair. The look on our faces when the two of them walked back carrying the small writing bureau with the drawers and doors that Auntie Audrey couldn't resist. Dad's idea of repacking the boot so that the bureau could fit in if Auntie Audrey's suitcase could be lashed to the roof even though we had no luggage rack. Two hundred metres down the road, the clatter and thump on the rear window and us four passengers turning around to see Auntie Audrey's clothes stretched out behind us on the tarmac like giant bunting. Blouses, skirts, sweaters, underwear, swimsuits. Reds and blues, whites and greens. A designer wake. And now here we were at a wake of a very different kind.

And soon the five of us would be going our separate ways. Gone were the two family homes only streets away from each other, replaced with five little flats. Three of them scattered like small nests, each in a different tree in a separate wood. Now the only two close to each other were Gus and Adrian, living in the same town. Sort of a couple again.

And I had reminded myself of the earlier days

of the "Rage Age" as Dad had called it. When both marriages were contaminating the other and slowly collapsing. And the anger, years after the event, when I had understood that I had been the unwitting fulcrum. That the only reason Mum and Dad had agreed I could go with Adrian and Audrey on their holiday to Portugal one year, was so that Adrian could show the Wife Who Never Wanted Children, that kids weren't necessarily all bad. And how the similarity in my movement to Uncle Adrian's, captured clearly in our holiday isolation, had been queried so cruelly by Audrey.

*

The other mourners had drifted away not long after Mum and Auntie Audrey left. When it was just the three of us, I suddenly felt tearful and took myself off to my room. I left Dad and Uncle Adrian in the hotel bar, reliving a boyhood encounter about a holiday in a dilapidated caravan on the Kent coast. I knew the story as well as they did. I paused out of their sight, at the top of the staircase, for the punch-line that I knew Uncle Adrian would soon be giving. Although I could not distinguish the words, the laughter and slapping of leatherette allowed me to go to bed in the comforting knowledge that some things never change.

I had lain awake thinking over the events of the previous few weeks and of the details I had heard from Mrs Barber and others earlier in the day. How Nan's death had been so sudden. How she had scuttled back from the baker's first thing in the morning with a warm baguette for her lunch with Betty Barber and been dead before noon. As soon as he had taken the call from Betty, Dad had telephoned Uncle Adrian and then me. It was touching that Dad had tried to sound measured when he said Nan had passed away in her favourite armchair, her dog-eared copy of The Decline and Fall of the Roman Empire, open on her lap. Poor old Mrs Barber had thought Nan was asleep, he'd said. In an ill-judged effort to soften the blow, he had wondered what Betty's already surprised face must have looked like when she found Nan. 'A better model for Edvard Munch than the amateur he used in that Scream painting,' Dad had said. It was only when I started to sob over the phone that he had joined in. As though he needed my permission.

I had thought of Betty's secret, shared with me that afternoon. How it was she who had brushed Nan's hair, placed her glasses on her head, taken down from the bookcase her favourite book and laid it on her lap.

*

And now today, I had arrived for breakfast before Dad and Uncle Adrian. They had shared a twin room and sauntered in a few minutes after me. Dad with his newspaper under his arm; Adrian with smart-phone in hand. Dad in a T-shirt; Adrian in his crisp, striped button-down. Their differences superficial, like varying varnish on otherwise matching sideboards. We were in no rush and all three of us lingered over the menu, willing prisoners to the breakfast smells drifting around the room; the sweet aroma of croissants jostling with the smell of grilled bacon; the sharp whiff of kippers as the waiter passed us en route to a ruddy-faced businessman at the window table, softly menacing someone via his mobile. In the end we decided to graze on the continental option.

Juices and fruit seemed the best antidotes to the intake of the previous evening.

'I thought that went as well as it could,' said Adrian through the last chewings of a peach.

'Yes, very civilised,' my Dad replied. 'And it was so nice to see old Betty Barber again. I think it took her a week to get over the shock.'

'When do you collect the ashes?' I asked of them both.

'In about two weeks,' they replied in perfect unison, looking at each other as if to say that hadn't happened for a while. It had, of course.

'I thought we'd scatter them on Ashdown Forest. She loved walking there.' My Dad said this with an edge that made it clear this was not just a suggestion but a firm proposition.

Adrian made a face, as though the apple juice he had just sipped had turned out to be someone's urine sample. 'Ashdown Forest? Come off it Gus. We've got to scatter them on Dad's grave. She'd want to be with him.'

'She would not Adrian. She'd made a whole life after he died. And we never really knew him. Why would we want to start trooping to some cemetery in Brighton? We never have before.'

Dad and Adrian were not good at arguing with each other. Neither wanted to best the other, but it was clear to me that they both felt strongly about this. And so the controlled tussle continued through coffee and toast. It made me sad, not only that they were squabbling, but because they were both wrong.

'I didn't mean a holiday Dad. I meant take Nan's ashes to Pompeii and scatter them there. The three of us.'

'Pompeii? Are you mad Laura?' said Dad. 'Why on earth would we take the ashes there? It's not as though any of us could visit more than once every couple of years.'

I placed my hand over my Dad's. 'It has to be Pompeii Dad. Don't you see, it's the placed she loved? She'll be at peace there. It's what Nan would have wanted. What do you think Uncle Adrian?'

They both looked at me. Dad's glare prompted by my invitation to Adrian to challenge his brother's view. Uncle Adrian's gaze was through me and as he explained later, through time, to a place where he recalled the groves of olives and lemons and the smell of vine tomatoes. Where donkeys, laden with fruit, could still be seen idling along dusty roads.

Uncle Adrian turned to face his brother. 'Do you remember the amphitheatre in Pompeii Gus? Where Mum did that silly dance for us and we joined in? What were we, nine and ten years old?'

Dad smiled, his nodding head confirming more than his total recall of that moment from their childhood. He slipped his right hand out from under mine and placed it on top, at the same time covering Adrian's hand with his left. The waiter approaching with a fresh pot of coffee, stopped short of our table, as though he had seen that a spell had been cast and was about to enchant all those present.

Life on the Edge

In the darkness, hat in hand, he prayed silently for forgiveness and for another successful burglary. His prayer over, Julio dabbed at the sweat on his face with the front of his open shirt. He listened to the last sounds of the construction site closing down for the weekend: the engine of the big flat-bed truck being started up; the calling and whooping of his work-mates as they clambered onto its dusty back; the clanging of the stout metal gates as they were slammed and secured; the truck driving away towards town with the sound of men singing, fading in time with the late afternoon light.

Julio waited another five minutes in his hiding place, breathing in the smell of lightly-oiled metal and listening out for any noise that may tell him there was someone still around. But the only sound was from a plane high overhead, inbound to Albuquerque International. He turned on his flashlight and took the few steps to the hut door.

'Hola mis bellezas,' he said looking fondly at the nuts securing the heavy lock to the outside of the door. 'I see like the others, you are made to stop people breaking in. Not breaking out. Gracias.'

Once outside, Julio hurried through the materials' compound with its stands of treated timber, towering over bundles of concrete pipes. He paused at the equipment rack and, with a metal on metal zing, slid out a ladder. As he made his way towards the perimeter fence, he was thinking that the haul in the pocket of his workpants would fetch $500. He began to hum the hymn that he and Margarita had chosen for their wedding ceremony. As he threaded his way through the huddle of silent site huts, he again marvelled at their quality, how they were better than any hut he had ever lived in. He gave a passing pat to the side of the canteen, which at lunch-times had the good sense to sit in the merciful shade of the new condo next to the site. He looked up at it now and froze. His mouth fell open. His breathing stopped. There on a narrow ledge, high up the condo, stood the figure of a young man. Julio counted the storeys. The boy was on the sixth floor.

Instinctively, Julio threw himself back and pressed his body hard against the hut wall, the dusty Albuquerque air now being sought in deep gulps. His mind had gone into freeze-frame until he realised that he was still carrying the ladder as a soldier carries a rifle and that the tip must be protruding like an antenna above the hut roof. He eased the ladder down before deciding he needed another look at the boy on the ledge. Julio stepped out from the shade of the hut and looked up again at the tall condo before him and the young man staring back down from between the pointy tips of his cowboy boots.

'What the hell are you doing there?' said the boy.

Julio looked around him for some sort of help but already knew that this elevation of the condominium, could only be seen from the construction site: the very reason he had planned his theft this way. He alone was witness to the scene. He licked his lips and swallowed.

'Senor, what is the problem? You must not be on this ledge. You must climb back inside your window.'

The young man looked down. 'You should have left for the weekend by now,' he called in a tone of annoyance that threw Julio yet further off balance. 'I've been waiting all afternoon for the site to empty. Please go. You don't need to see this.'

'But Senor, what is the problem? What are you trying to do? What can be so bad that you are going to end your life?'

'Please, just go.'

Julio's brain whirled. If the boy jumped, his body would be found when site security did their patrol tonight, Saturday at the latest. That would make this place a much bigger crime scene than Julio had allowed for. But if the boy climbed back inside the window, he might call Albuquerque's finest. Julio did not know which was worse. But he knew one thing. That God had not heard his prayer.

'My name is Julio. Do you mind if I ask you something...?'

'Kendall,' yelled the young man. 'My name is Kendall Walters.'

'Senor Kendall, is so hot down here. And my throat is so dry, shouting to you is painful. Could I come to your apartment please, for some water?'

'The door's open Julio,' said Kendall, his tone now calmer. 'But if I'm not here when you arrive, help yourself to whatever.'

Julio toppled the ladder as he jumped from the fence and landed outside in a sprinter's crouch. He raced towards the entrance of the condominium, the sign above whose grand entrance doors declared it to be "Santa Fe Heights". A banner hung down confirming the Show Apartment was Now Open for Viewing. He never gave a thought to the gleaming bank of elevators, but raced up the marbled stairs two at a time. His breath came in large gulps as he arrived at the open door to apartment 601.

From where he stood in the doorway, Julio looked across a dining area to Kendall's back pressed hard against the window. He took it all in with a single glance. Furniture and decorations that he had only seen in magazines or at the movies. A table set for four with a vase of extravagant silk flowers at its centre. White surfaces broken up with splashes and clashes of colour. Modern artwork around the walls. A gaudy chandelier hanging above it all, like a steel vulture in flight.

'I am here Senor Kendall and I am glad you are also.' Julio moved to the window and the well-dressed back of Kendall Walters.

'Senor Kendall, please step back inside. What could be so bad that you choose to die?'

'It's complicated Julio, but... this is the only way. This thing's been building for weeks and it's all going to blow on Monday morning.'

'What thing Senor?'

'Oh, a little matter of $600 million that I have just lost the Bank of New Mexico.' Julio gave the low whistle of an appreciative accomplice.

'Yes, that's a little more than whatever it was you just stole from the hut down there I think.'

Julio traced the shape of the diamond-tipped drill bits in the pocket of his cargo pants. It had been his plan to make this job the last one. This was the third time it had worked, but after tonight the company would surely realise it was not someone breaking in, but someone hiding on site and breaking out. He had planned to wait a few weeks and then leave the construction site and move to another. Somewhere else where they weren't too fussy about papers and work permits. There were plenty in Albuquerque. Julio scraped one of the dining chairs across the tiled floor and sat down facing Kendall's back.

'Tell me more Senor Kendall, about what you have done. Why cannot you just own up? Nobody died eh?'

'Well Julio, you may not have heard of derivatives, but I have been buying and selling and hedging my way to this $600 million loss over the last two months.' He looked down at the near one hundred foot drop. 'Now, it's all gone. Kerash!'

'So it is a bit like gambling Senor Kendall?'

'It IS gambling Julio. Snuck up on me. I've never so much as put a dollar on a horse before.'

'So you know about banks, but not about gambling? Me, I am the other way around.'

So Julio, you are a gambler as well as a thief?'

Julio stiffened as though the heavy hand of a police officer had gripped his sweat-patched collar. It was a stupid question from the boy and he paused while he bit back his anger. He thought of the $100 he had to send home to Mexico every week, just so that Margarita and the boys could survive. Every week was a gamble. Every week a different risk. Often he had to go hungry himself so that they did not. And getting caught would mean gaol and deportation. And deportation meant a return to penury. He looked up at the ceiling in frustration and then once more let his gaze take in the room. And there on the table, beside the vase of extravagant silk flowers, lay a single sheet of paper. How could he have missed it? He leaned over and silently lifted the note, as a worshipper might lift a hymn sheet once the music had started. For he knew at once, that he could let the boy jump. The existence of a suicide note meant the police would not be looking for anyone else. Silently, he began to read.

'So what's your answer Julio, gambler as well as a thief?'

'Yes, I think I have been both thief and gambler for some years Senor,' Julio said without looking up. 'But you are new to both no?'

'Hold on now Julio, I'm not a thief, I never stole anything in my life. I'm a damn fool gambler, but not a thief.'

'But don't you say you lose the bank's money and gave it to someone else and the bank don't know yet? That sounds like a thief thing to me. And maybe you pay for your fancy apartment with their money too eh?'

Julio was still looking at the note. It was to the boy's father, who also seemed to work for the same bank as his son. He was apologising for letting the old man down. Stressing that all his attempts to recoup the growing losses had been well-meant, but accepting now they were madness. Asking his father to say goodbye and sorry to his mother. Julio looked up when Kendall replied.

'Well Julio, first off it's not my apartment. It's the Show Apartment. I viewed it on Tuesday and told the agent I wanted to view it again. He loaned me the keys. Far as I know, the rest of the block is empty. Second of all I gambled, not stole, the bank's money. But either way it is not coming back. So I intend to jump. Sure, I know it's the coward's way out.' His voice dropped to a murmur. 'And I know it will break Ma's heart.'

The relaxed tone that Kendall had first adopted had slipped away, like a little boat slipping its mooring. The back of his tailored shirt was stuck to the window with sweat. Julio was imagining the sucking sound Kendall would make when he jumped, as the young man continued.

'I've written a note to my father. Believe me, he will prefer me to do this rather than shame him. 'Til he retired, he was President of the Bank. He's besotted with the bank. He'll think jumping was honourable. If he was sitting where you are, he'd reach out and push me.'

Maybe I should give old man Walters a call, thought Julio, time is dragging on. But then again I can see that fat wallet in the back pocket of your pants and it would be a shame for all that to go down with you. Maybe I should drag you in and beat you to death with it. I could then spend the murder weapon and we'd both be happy.

'So Senor, you wrote to your father. That is good. But you want me to give a message to anyone else? Maybe your girl. She be very sad when she find she lose a fine boy like you.'

'Very kind Julio, but I don't have a girl. Not now. She walked three months ago when she thought the job was more important to me than she was. It wasn't. But I never told her that.'

Yet another plane bound for Albuquerque

International glided silently across the purpling sky. From where Julio sat, it appeared to pass right through Kendall's head. In one ear and out the other. At that moment, the back of the young man reminded him of his own eldest son Javier, when he would stand on the end of the jetty looking at the stars, in the days before the little fishing boat was repossessed. How all his gentle calling to the boy would go unheeded until Javier had finished making his silent wish.

Slowly shaking his head from side to side, Julio laid down the suicide note. He took out from the breast pocket of his work-shirt, the drill-bit docket he had put there less than an hour ago.

'Ah yes, I see your note to your father Senor Kendall.' Julio rustled the docket. 'Mmm, no, no, no. This is shit. I get rid of it. Better your family see no note than this one.'

'Wha' wha' now wait a minute Julio. You leave that note right where it is. I mean, put it back on the table, damn it!'

Julio stood and started to scrunch the docket

noisily into a ball as he walked to within Kendall's peripheral vision. He ceremoniously placed the screwed up ball of paper into his mouth and started munching. 'Senor Kendall, you're suicide note even tastes like shit,' he mumbled.

'You crazy bastard. How could you eat a man's suicide note? How…'

Julio held up one hand like a traffic cop and placed the other on his chest. He swallowed down the last of the docket and let out a long burp. The noise reminded him of the low growl with which a guard-dog had once greeted him on a locked construction site in Tres Cruces.

'Don't worry Senor Kendall. We can write you another. We need to write a note where we tell your folks how much you love them, how much you appreciated what they have done for you and that they must not pine over your passing. A nice suicide note. A proper suicide note.'

The roar of a reply seemed to come up from Kendall's hand-made Texan boots, 'WE?'

'Well, Senor Kendall, I don't see how you can write this note on your own while you are out there on the ledge.'

'You miserable sonofabitch. There should be no new note. The one I wrote said it all.'

'OK, Senor Kendall, but that is what we have here. If you don't need my help to write it, why don't I just pass out a piece of paper and a pen? You can do another all on your own.'

'Damn right. Steal from your employer then steal a man's suicide note. Sonofabitch. So, go find me a pen and some card or something to write on.'

Kendall's beautifully tailored suit jacket was hanging on the back of one of the chairs, as though the wearer had gone to the water-cooler. In the inside pocket, Julio found a screw-top fountain pen. From the Show House brochure sitting on the breakfast bar, he tore the back cover. He walked to the open window and said quietly, 'Here you are Senor Kendall, the pen first.'

Kendall put his hand inside the window. Julio grabbed it.